From Me to You

To my Pa, Andrea, who told me things.
To my children, Antia and Timothy, to whom I told things.
And to their children, who will be told interesting things.
AB

For Trevor, my Dad. JB

First American Edition 2019
Kane Miller, A Division of EDC Publishing

Text Copyright © Anthony Bertini 2018
Illustrations Copyright © Jonathan Bentley 2018

First published in Australia in 2018 by Little Hare Books, an imprint of Hardie Grant Egmont

For information contact:
Kane Miller, A Division of EDC Publishing
P.O. Box 470663
Tulsa, OK 74147-0663
www.kanemiller.com
www.edcpub.com
www.usbornebooksandmore.com

Library of Congress Control Number: 2018958287

Printed and bound in China
1 2 3 4 5 6 7 8 9 10
ISBN: 978-1-61067-903-9

The illustrations in this book were created using pencil and watercolors.

From Me to You

Kane Miller
A DIVISION OF EDC PUBLISHING

You still fit in a box.

Easily lost in a crowd.

You have yet to grow
your two front teeth.

Your shoes are too big.

You will grow into
your clothes.

You fear the dark,

hate it when dogs growl.

Rain doesn't stop you.

Everyone is your friend.

You cry easily,
smile just as fast.
Your anger is soon gone.

Small is all you know.

Time will come soon
enough to be big.

Big is exciting.

Everything seems possible.

Big is an adventure.

And life will teach you
to be brave.

You will fail many times.

But you will overcome disappointment.

Your scars will heal.

You will learn to jump high.

Fortune may come,

fortune may go.

You were born perfect.

And it is up to you to stay that way.

Listen to your heart.

Take wise counsel.

Assemble the maps.
But set your own compass.

You will be big most
of your life.

Enjoy this brief time,
just you and me.

Our days together
are short.

Sometime soon,
you will just be you.

Your shoes will fit.

Your arms will reach.

You will find the key.

I will stay in your heart.
Watching along the way.